The River

BOOKS BY JEZ BUTTERWORTH
PUBLISHED BY TCG

Jerusalem

Mojo and Other Plays

INCLUDES:

Leavings

Mojo

The Naked Eye

The Night Heron

Parlour Song

The Winterling

.The River

Jez Butterworth

THEATRE COMMUNICATIONS GROUP
NEW YORK
2014

"After Moonless Midnight" from *River: Poems by Ted Hughes* (1983, new edition 2011), and "Burnt Norton" from *Four Quartets* by T. S. Eliot (1944) both published by Faber and Faber Ltd

The River is published by Theatre Communications Group, Inc., 520 Eighth Avenue, 24th Floor, New York, NY 10018-4156

This volume is published in arrangement with Nick Hern Books Lim- ited, The Glasshouse, 49a Goldhawk Road, London, W12 8QP

This publication is made possible in part by the New York State Council on the Arts with the support of Governor Andrew Cuomo and the New York State Legislature.

TCG books are exclusively distributed to the book trade by Consortium Book Sales and Distribution.

A catalogue record for this book is available from the Library of Congress.

ISBN 978-1-55936-488-1 (paperback)

Cover design by: feastcreative.com

First TCG Edition, October 2014

The River was first produced by the Royal Court, London at the Jerwood Theatre Upstairs, from October 18, 2012 to November 17, 2012 with the following cast (in order of appearance):

Dominic West

Miranda Raison

Laura Donnelly

Director   Ian Rickson

Designer   Ultz

Lighting Designer   Charles Balfour

Sound Designer   Ian Dickinson for Autograph

Composer   Stephen Warbeck

The River received its North American premiere at the Circle in the Square Theatre, New York on November 16, 2014 (previews from October 31) with the following cast (in order of appearance):

Hugh Jackman

Cush Jumbo

Laura Donnelly

Director   Ian Rickson

Designer   Ultz

Lighting Designer   Charles Balfour

Sound Designer   Ian Dickinson for Autograph

Composer   Stephen Warbeck

US Casting   Jim Carnahan, CSA

The Royal Court Theatre production was produced by

Sonia Friedman Productions

Stuart Thompson, Scott Rudin, Roger Berlind,

Colin Callender, Scott Landis, Tulchin Bartner Productions

in association with JFL Theatricals, 1001 Nights

The River

For Joanna Butterworth (1964–2012).
All our love, for ever.

'At the still point of the turning world. Neither flesh nor fleshless;
Neither from nor towards; at the still point, there the dance is,
But neither arrest nor movement. And do not call it fixity,
Where past and future are gathered. Neither movement from nor
    towards,
Neither ascent nor decline. Except for the point, the still point,
There would be no dance, and there is only the dance.'

T. S. Eliot, 'Burnt Norton', Four Quartets

6

Characters

THE MAN
THE WOMAN
THE OTHER WOMAN

Setting

The cabin on the cliffs, above the river.

Note on Text

A forward slash (/) indicates interrupted speech.

Darkness. The river.

Becomes...

...A cabin. Door off to bedroom at the back. Table. Chairs. Stove. Sink. Spiders. A WOMAN*'s voice, singing, off.*

WOMAN'S VOICE (*singing*).
>I went out to a hazel wood
>Because a fire was in my head
>And cut and peeled a hazel wand
>And hooked a berry to a thread...

Enter THE WOMAN, *from the bedroom.*

THE WOMAN (*singing*).
>And when white moths were on the wing
>And moth-like stars were flickering out
>I dropped the berry in the stream
>And caught a little silver trout...

She turns, and looks towards the window. Stops.

Here. (*Calls.*) Quick! Come here. Don't miss this. Quickly.

Enter THE MAN, *carrying assorted fly-fishing equipment.*

THE MAN (*to himself*). Torch. Reel. Spare reel. Leader. Fly-box. Flies...

THE WOMAN. Quickly. You must see this.

THE MAN. Forceps. Scotch. Baccy. Gink. Priest. Where's my priest?

THE WOMAN. You are missing the most incredible thing.

THE MAN. Where's it gone? It was right here. Here in this drawer. Where's it gone?

THE WOMAN. Just stop what you're doing and come here now.

THE MAN. What?

THE WOMAN. Now. Right now. Come over here.

THE MAN. Oh. I've seen it.

Beat.

THE WOMAN. What?

THE MAN. I've seen it before.

THE WOMAN. It's never happened before.

THE MAN. Yes it has.

THE WOMAN. No it hasn't. Not like this.

THE MAN. Just like that. They're all the same.

THE WOMAN. No two sunsets are the same.

THE MAN. Have you seen my priest?

THE WOMAN. Describe it.

THE MAN. It's a small piece of ram's horn with a leather
    handle, about yay big with –

THE WOMAN. Describe the sunset. If you've seen it before –

THE MAN. We don't have time.

THE WOMAN. Before anything else happens. Before this relation-
    ship moves on one inch. Describe it. Describe my sunset.

They look at each other.

THE MAN (*to himself*). August. Low cloud. (*Aloud.*) Blood red
    as far as the headland turning to lilac-blue wisps above the
    bluff. Trails of apricot, feathering out through blue, dark
    blue, and aquamarine to an iris ring of obsidian and above
    that the Evening Star. (*Finds it.*) Yes! You little beauty.
    (*Holds it up.*) See that? That's a priest. We're all set.

THE WOMAN. Thank you. That was a magical moment. I'm
    so glad we could share it.

THE MAN. What did I do?

THE WOMAN. It's little moments like that which make life
    special isn't it? "That evening at the cabin. When they

watched the sunset. Our sunset he called it. And she remembered the moment for ever."

THE MAN. Why aren't you dressed?

THE WOMAN. I'm not coming.

THE MAN. What?

THE WOMAN. I have sunburn. And my book just got good.

THE MAN. What's the date today?

THE WOMAN. *To the Lighthouse*.

THE MAN. August 21st.

THE WOMAN. Virginia Woolf.

THE MAN. What does that make tomorrow?

THE WOMAN. It's about these people who go to a lighthouse...

THE MAN. August 22nd.

THE WOMAN. Or do they? Will they actually make it...

THE MAN. Which is...?

THE WOMAN. To the lighthouse...?

THE MAN. The New Moon! Tonight there's no moon. It's warm. Cumulus cloud. Big sunset –

THE WOMAN. You don't say?

THE MAN. Once a year, when there's no moon. Late summer, when the river's in spate, that's when they move. The sea trout. The sea trout are running! The storm last night. No rain for weeks. The pools get low, then whoosh! A million tons of water drops from the sky. In one night. They're out there, right now, with no moon, a neap tide –

THE WOMAN. Look. You / tried to –

THE MAN. This happens / once every year.

THE WOMAN. You tried to teach me –

THE MAN (*interrupting*). Once!

THE WOMAN. You tried to teach me to cast all day on the beach. All I did was make knots. I couldn't do it in broad / daylight.

THE MAN. It's easy. You / just feel it.

THE WOMAN. How am I going to do it in the pitch bloody dark.

THE MAN (*interrupting*). There are monsters out there. Huge monsters. In the water. Right now!

THE WOMAN. You're really selling this.

Pause.

THE MAN. The table's moved.

THE WOMAN. What?

THE MAN. What? No I was just –

THE WOMAN. I can move it back.

THE MAN. No, it's fine. I was just saying… I don't know why. It's no big deal.

THE WOMAN. I'll move it back.

THE MAN. What? Don't.

THE WOMAN. It's the work of a moment. Here. (*Picks it up.*) Oww.

THE MAN. What's wrong? Are you okay.

THE WOMAN. I'm fine.

THE MAN. Show me.

THE WOMAN. It's just a splinter.

THE MAN. Let me look at it.

THE WOMAN. Ow.

THE MAN. Let me see.

THE WOMAN. It's a splinter.

THE MAN. Show me it.

THE WOMAN. I said I'm fine.

THE MAN. It's bleeding. Come here. Let me see. (*Takes her hand*.) That's deep.

He takes out a knife.

THE WOMAN. What are you doing?

THE MAN. I'm going to get it out.

THE WOMAN. Not with that you're not…

THE MAN. Trust me.

She holds out her hand.

Ready?

THE WOMAN. Wait. The other end. It went in this way.

THE MAN. Keep still. Ready.

THE WOMAN. Fuck it.

THE MAN. Ready. Steady.

THE WOMAN. Ow.

He pulls it out.

THE MAN. Now suck it.

THE WOMAN. I'm sucking it.

THE MAN. Suck it hard.

THE WOMAN. Stop saying that. I'm sucking it.

THE MAN. I'll put a plaster on it.

THE WOMAN. I don't need a plaster. Besides, I deserved it.

THE MAN. What?

THE WOMAN. I never should have moved it.

THE MAN. Look –

THE WOMAN. New girlfriend. Shows up. Moves the table –

THE MAN. Look I don't –

THE WOMAN. First time here. *Moves the table.*

THE MAN. Okay –

THE WOMAN. No warning. Just… moves it.

THE MAN. Look –

THE WOMAN. By the way I used a teabag earlier. I hope that's ok. I also took a dead spider out of your coffee pot.

THE MAN. To be absolutely clear, I don't care if you move the table. I don't care if you break a glass. I don't care if you smash a window or accidentally burn the cabin to the ground with me inside. I do care if you don't come with me, now, to the – (*Stops.*) Wait. Wait there. (*Heads to a small bookshelf.*) There. (*Pulls book out, flicks pages.*) Wait. Wait. Wait there. Don't move. (*Stops.*) Here. Read this. Just read that. And if after you've read it, you don't want to come, you don't have to. Deal? But read it. Read the poem. Read it aloud.

THE WOMAN. You want me to read this aloud.

THE MAN. Read the title.

THE WOMAN. Aloud.

THE MAN. Yes.

BOTH (*she reads*). 'After / Moonless Midnight.'

THE MAN. '*After* Moonless Midnight.' 'After Moonless Midnight.' Okay. Now read it.

THE WOMAN. Do you mind? I'm / trying to rea–

THE MAN. Okay just read it.

THE WOMAN. May I? (*Pause.*) 'After Moonless Midnight.' By… (*Looks at cover. Makes face.*) Hmm…

THE MAN. Wait. Stop. (*Beat.*) What do you mean? What's that supposed to mean?

THE WOMAN. What? Nothing. What did I do?

THE MAN. Give it back.

THE WOMAN. I'm reading it.

THE MAN. Give it back.

THE WOMAN. I'm reading the poem.

THE MAN. Forget it. It won't work.

THE WOMAN. Why not?

THE MAN.…No. It's not going to work –

THE WOMAN. Says who?

THE MAN. Forget it. Okay. (*Beat.*) Hmmm… You went – (*Turns the book over.*) and then you went 'Hmmm…'

THE WOMAN. So now I can't / go 'Hmmmm…'

THE MAN. No, not 'Hmmmm'. 'Hmmmm…'

THE WOMAN. And what does 'Hmmmm' mean?

THE MAN. 'And what does "Hmmmm" mean? Give me / the book.'

THE WOMAN. How dare you say I won't get it? You have the balls to stand there in those silly rubber wellies and accuse me –

THE MAN. I'm not accusing anyone. It's perfectly okay. If you're not open to it…

THE WOMAN. Excuse me?

THE MAN. What?

THE WOMAN. 'Not open to it'…

THE MAN. Give me the book.

THE WOMAN. As in closed.

THE MAN. I never said you were closed.

THE WOMAN. In what sense is not open not closed?

THE MAN. This is now ridiculous.

THE WOMAN. I spent several hours today standing on a beach in the blazing sunshine trying to cast, I tied knots. The Arbor knot. The Davy knot. The Double Surgeon. I learned the names of the flies, wet flies, dry flies. Nymphs. Droppers. I'm not closed. I'm sunburned. My book just got good. And you wouldn't look at my sodding sunset!

Pause.

THE MAN. There's a long pool. Just past the bridge, just past the rapids where the path runs steep. The river suddenly plunges thirty-feet deep over black stones. I went out this morning. I climbed the cliff and looked down from the track above the pool. Deep in the river. Lined up in shoals. Like U-boats. Silver. Resting. Thirty or forty of them. The most beautiful, shyest, fiercest creatures… Huge. Waiting. Ready to run. And if you catch one… if you catch one, it's like catching a lightning bolt. It's like jamming your finger into a socket. Like a million sunsets rolled into a ball and shot straight into your veins. And you feel it. By God, you feel it. I've overdone this.

THE WOMAN. Show me the poem.

THE MAN. No…

THE WOMAN. I want to / read the poem.

THE MAN. No. It's – No. It doesn't matter.

THE WOMAN. Hang on a minute –

THE MAN. No, it's not a big deal. It wasn't supposed to be a / big –

THE WOMAN. Oh no you don't. No you don't.

THE MAN. What?

THE WOMAN. No you don't, chum. I'm not the one he took to his cabin who got sunburn. Splinter Girl. The Table-Mover. I want to be shaken to my core. I want a million lightning bolts shot up my arse. Give me the poem.

THE MAN. Honestly you / don't have to.

THE WOMAN. Give me the poem.

THE MAN. It's your holiday…

THE WOMAN. Then give me the poem.

He looks at her. He gives her the poem.

(*Reads.*) 'After Moonless Midnight.

I waded, deepening, and the fish
Listened for me. They watched my each move
Through their magical skins. In the stillness
Their eyes waited, furious with gold brightness,
Their gills moved. And in their thick sides
The power waited. And in their torpedo
Concentration, their mouth-aimed intent
Their savagery waited, and their explosion.
They waited for me... The whole river
Listened to me... and, blind,
Invisibly watched me. And held me deeper
With its blind invisible hands
"We've got him" it whispered. "We've got him".'

They look at each other.

Darkness.

The river, rushing.

The cabin. Lit by a paraffin lamp. THE MAN, *fishing jacket, pacing, alone. Sweating. Dialing a number on his phone.*

THE MAN. Hello. Hello? (*Looks at his phone. Bad signal. Shakes it. Finds a place to stand where it works. Dials again.*) Hello? Police. Someone is missing. A woman. She went to the river. We were fishing. There's no moon. I lost her. In the dark. Hello? (*Looks at it.*) Fuck. (*Rage.*) Fuck it. (*Bangs it on the table. Puts it to his ear.*) Hello? (*Beat.*) Yes. Hello? Hello? Who's – ? Who are – ? I was talking to a woman. A police... (*Beat.*) Okay. Sir. (*Beat.*) Between St Crispin's and the Long Pool. The long stretch under the oak trees. Yes. (*Beat.*) I don't know. It was pitch dark. I called and called. (*Listens.*) She's thirty. About five six, slim build. She's wearing a... my fishing jacket. My old fishing jacket. It's green. And –

A door bangs offstage.

Wait. Wait there. Hold on. (*Calls.*) Who is it? Is that you?

WOMAN'S VOICE (*off*). Here!

THE MAN. Thank Christ.

WOMAN'S VOICE (*off*). Quick come see!

THE MAN. Thank fuck. (*Into phone*.) Sorry. I'm sorry. She's back. False alarm. I'm extremely sorry. Thank you. Thank you. (*Hangs up. Closes eyes*.) Thank you.

Enter THE OTHER WOMAN. *She stands in the lantern glow.*

Where have you been? I've been looking for you for two hours. Where the fuck were you?

THE OTHER WOMAN. I was down by the river.

THE MAN. Where by the river?

THE OTHER WOMAN. Where you left me.

THE MAN. I looked there.

THE OTHER WOMAN. Well / that's where I was.

THE MAN. I shouted and shouted. Where were you?

THE OTHER WOMAN. Where were you?

THE MAN. I called the police.

THE OTHER WOMAN. What? Why?

THE MAN. I've been talking to the fucking… Just now.

THE OTHER WOMAN. The police?!

THE MAN. They were going to send a fucking helicopter. I was shouting and shouting. Up and down for two hours.

THE OTHER WOMAN. I got bored.

THE MAN. What?

THE OTHER WOMAN. I was just standing there in the dark. It was boring. I went for a walk.

THE MAN. Where?

THE OTHER WOMAN. Up the river.

THE MAN. And you didn't tell me.

THE OTHER WOMAN. I couldn't find you.

THE MAN. You fucking idiot.

THE OTHER WOMAN *laughs. He goes to hug her.*

I'm sorry. I was so worried.

THE OTHER WOMAN. I'm sorry. I didn't mean to scare –

THE MAN. I just… I thought something – I thought… Are you okay. You look pale.

THE OTHER WOMAN. I'm fine.

THE MAN. Your eyes are red. Have you been crying?

THE OTHER WOMAN. Do I look like I've been crying?

THE MAN. You look like you've been crying.

THE OTHER WOMAN. I haven't been crying.

THE MAN. Whiskey. I need a whiskey. *You* need a whiskey. We need whiskey. (*Starts searching cupboards.*) Where's the fucking whiskey? It was right here. Here in this drawer. Where the fuck's it gone? I can't believe you didn't hear me. I was shouting for hours.

THE OTHER WOMAN. I didn't hear you. Did you hear me?

THE MAN. What? When?

THE OTHER WOMAN. Shouting.

THE MAN. When.

THE OTHER WOMAN. By the river. I was shouting too.

THE MAN. Where? When?

THE OTHER WOMAN. So you didn't hear.

THE MAN. Wait. Stop. Why were you shouting? If nothing was wrong why were you shouting. If you weren't hurt or being eaten by a wolf or… drowning… If everything was fine, why were you shouting?

THE OTHER WOMAN. I'll show you.

She reaches in her bag and pulls out an enormous sea trout. Three pounds. Slaps it on the table.

THE MAN. Where did you get that?

THE OTHER WOMAN. I'll give you three guesses.

THE MAN. Fuck me. She's enormous.

THE OTHER WOMAN. She? She's a girl?

THE MAN. A grilse. She's straight from the sea.

THE OTHER WOMAN. That's right. A grilse. That's what Danny said she was.

THE MAN. Jesus! (*Stops.*) Danny? Who's Danny?

THE OTHER WOMAN. A fisherman.

THE MAN. Where?

THE OTHER WOMAN. By the river. I met him in the dark. Nice bloke. He helped me land him. Her.

THE MAN. He helped you.

THE OTHER WOMAN. Yes.

Beat.

THE MAN. Well, good for him. You were lucky then. They're not easy to land. Not for a novice. Not alone. Jesus. It must be three pounds.

THE OTHER WOMAN. Three pounds three-and-a-half ounces. Danny weighed it.

Beat.

THE MAN. Did he.

THE OTHER WOMAN. He was really helpful. Danny said the sea trout have been shy all summer. He's a plumber. And a drummer. But he's thinking of leaving. The singer's a prat. So we had a chat. Then we shared a quick spliff. Then Danny took a look at that thing you tied on the end of my rod, that orange thingy. What was it called?

THE MAN. An Orange Darter.

THE OTHER WOMAN. Right. He cut that off and put on something else.

THE MAN. What? What did he put on?

THE OTHER WOMAN. A Monster Munch.

Beat.

THE MAN. A Monster Munch?

THE OTHER WOMAN. Pickled onion. Just stuck it on a hook. Then he stood behind me and helped me cast it. And I bunged it in… and ten seconds later, bingo. It felt like I'd shut my sleeve in a bus. It jerked my heart up into my mouth and I suddenly needed to pee. That's me, if something incredible happens, I suddenly need to pee.

THE MAN. A Monster Munch?

THE OTHER WOMAN. Instantly. I'm a big pee-er at key moments. If I'm suddenly so excited I don't know what to do or say that's when I instantly need to pee. It's ruined some great moments.

THE MAN. That's not fishing. That's poaching. A Monster Munch? That's fucking poaching.

THE OTHER WOMAN. They went mad for them. Danny caught loads.

THE MAN. He's not even supposed to be fishing there.

THE OTHER WOMAN. He mentioned that.

THE MAN. That's my uncle's water. That whole stretch for two miles. No one else can fish it. Not without permission. And certainly not with a pickled-onion fucking Monster Munch.

Beat.

THE OTHER WOMAN. So how did you get on? Any luck?

Beat.

THE MAN. Quiet.

THE OTHER WOMAN. Quiet.

THE MAN. Quiet.

THE OTHER WOMAN. But 'twas a moonless night.

THE MAN. And I spent half of it looking for you. What did he look like?

THE OTHER WOMAN. Search me. It was dark. Like a fisherman.

THE MAN. Poacher. Not a fisherman. Not Danny the Fisherman. Danny the Poacher.

THE OTHER WOMAN. You're jealous.

THE MAN. You're stoned. I'm not jealous.

THE OTHER WOMAN. You look jealous…

THE MAN. You look stoned. Your eyes are bright red.

THE OTHER WOMAN. Me and a stranger. Together in the dark. Holding the rod together. Close. Whispering to each other. Then all that thrashing about.

THE MAN. Did he touch you?

THE OTHER WOMAN. He was teaching me to fish.

THE MAN. I bet he was…

THE OTHER WOMAN. *Schooling* me. Showing me the ropes.

THE MAN. I bet he was.

THE OTHER WOMAN Out there by the river. Out there in the black.

THE MAN. Did you touch him?

THE OTHER WOMAN. I kissed him.

THE MAN. Why did you kiss him?

THE OTHER WOMAN. I kissed him goodbye.

THE MAN. How?

THE OTHER WOMAN. Like this.

She comes over and kisses him lightly on the cheek.

THE MAN. Like that.

THE OTHER WOMAN. And then I gave him a blowjob.

Pause.

THE MAN. But that's all.

THE OTHER WOMAN. We'd only just met. I have boundaries. So what do we do now?

THE MAN. Now?

THE OTHER WOMAN. With her. With the fish. With my fish.

THE MAN. Well, we can't exactly throw it back.

THE OTHER WOMAN. So what do we do?

THE MAN. We cook it. And we eat it.

Pause.

THE OTHER WOMAN. Can we do that?

THE MAN. Who's going to stop us?

THE OTHER WOMAN. Oh my God. We can can't we. We can just… Fuck!

THE MAN. What?

THE OTHER WOMAN (*starts to laugh*). That's ridiculous. One minute it was in its world. And now it's in ours. And now we're going to eat it. (*Stops.*) Oh my God. It's terrible. The world is terrible. But amazing. So fucking amazing. It's just I… I am… I am so so so so… fucking stoned right now… (*Beat.*) Seriously though. We can just eat it. That's incredible. That's… That's –

THE MAN. I love you.

Silence.

THE OTHER WOMAN. Don't be silly. You can't love me. I'm a poacher.

THE MAN. Come here.

THE OTHER WOMAN. I can't.

THE MAN. Why not.

THE OTHER WOMAN. I need to pee. (*Beat*.) Here's the plan. I'll go next door. Pee. Get it together. Come back and we'll take it from there. Agreed.

THE MAN. Agreed.

THE OTHER WOMAN. Thank you.

THE MAN. What for?

THE OTHER WOMAN. For calling the police. I like that you did that.

THE MAN. Why?

THE OTHER WOMAN. Because it means you were scared. I find that incredibly sexy. Were you really scared?

Pause.

THE MAN. I was terrified.

She exits into the bedroom.

He puts on some music. He takes a knife and guts the fish. He puts the fish in the oven. Pulls a cork, then chops some vegetables. Looks at his watch. Opens the little oven. Puts it in.

Do you want wine or whiskey?

WOMAN'S VOICE (*off*). You choose.

He pours a glass. The door opens. It's THE WOMAN. Dressed. Towelling her hair. He hands her the wine.

THE WOMAN. I forgot to say. When I came back from my walk this evening there was a robin in here. Little bird flying madly about, desperate, trying to find a way out. I opened all the windows but I forgot to open that one up high and it flew right into it. It fell right here on the floor.

THE MAN. Was it dead?

THE WOMAN. I don't know. I put it on a tea towel and carried it outside. I forgot to check if it's still there.

THE MAN. You can check in the morning.

THE WOMAN. I gave it a saucer of water.

THE MAN. It's happened before. It will be fine.

THE WOMAN. I hope so. Poor thing.

Beat.

THE MAN. Cheers.

THE WOMAN. Cheers.

THE MAN. Where did you walk? This evening.

THE WOMAN. I walked along the upper road. There's an old deserted house up there, at the end of the track. Right on the cliff before it drops down to the river. You've got to watch your step round the back wall. And there, standing on the slope, was this horse. Jet black. I approached it but it bolted away over the crest. I walked down the track. Into the village. I went into the graveyard. I read the names on the stones. One of the names was Greenhorn. That's an old family name. My grandmother's maiden name. There's a whole family buried there, in the 1900s, and all the children are under ten years old when they died. Six children, all dead. What must have that been like. Then the strangest thing happened.

THE MAN. What?

THE WOMAN. It was going dark, and I heard this whirring above, and right overhead, three white swans flew over. Low through the yew trees. The wind rose up so I headed home. Back through the woods. Along the river. By the river I lost the path. It gets quite tangled underfoot. I was concentrating on not falling over, or falling in, when suddenly I looked up. And I saw something.

THE MAN. What did you see?

THE WOMAN. I saw a woman. Standing by the water. Standing among the trees. About fifty feet away. She was about my age. She wasn't wearing a coat, or shoes. I called to her. 'Hello!' She looked at me. She didn't blink. I didn't know if she'd heard me so I called again. She pointed at me and she started to laugh. She laughed and laughed. The air was very still. Then she stopped, and though she was some way away, I heard her sigh. And she shook her head. And she turned and walked away. Then it started to rain so I hurried back.

He places the fish in front of her. Sits.

THE MAN. She'll be from the village. It's the start of the cider season. She was probably drunk on cider.

THE WOMAN. She didn't look drunk. I got soaked on the way back. Frozen through. When I got back here you weren't here. So I had a shot of whiskey and I waited for you.

THE MAN. Are you ready?

THE WOMAN. Ready.

They eat.

/ It's incredible.

THE MAN. Have you ever tasted / anything like that.

THE WOMAN. That is amazing. The flavour.

THE MAN. Go all over the world. Try any fish in any sea, lake, river or stream. A sea trout... A wild sea trout. (*Beat.*) So come on. How was it?

THE WOMAN. How was what?

THE MAN. When it took. When you hooked it. That first bite.

THE WOMAN. Oh come on. It was a complete fluke. I just bunged it in.

THE MAN. Rubbish. You hooked it. And got it in.

THE WOMAN. It gave me the fright of my life. When it took. It was like electricity. I've never felt anyth–

THE MAN. Did you feel it –

THE WOMAN. In the knees.

THE MAN. The stomach –

THE WOMAN. You can't move your feet.

THE MAN. The heart –

THE WOMAN. On fire.

THE MAN. Hammer blows –

THE WOMAN. And giddy.

THE MAN. Sick with goosebumps.

THE WOMAN. Dark and silent and you can hear each breath
   and every hoot and crow and creak and mole and –

THE MAN. Every scurry scuffle in the dark.

THE WOMAN. And you cast out into the black and you count
   and you pray and you don't know what you're doing and
   suddenly… suddenly it answers. It's just so… suddenly…
   fucking… real.

THE MAN. Incredible.

THE WOMAN. Absolutely totally… (*Beat*.) Yeah. (*Pause*.)
   Look. I have a horrible confession to make.

THE MAN. What?

THE WOMAN. I've done it before.

   He stops.

THE MAN. What? (*Beat*.) When?

THE WOMAN. Before.

THE MAN. When?

THE WOMAN. I'm sorry.

THE MAN. Who with?

THE WOMAN. My dad.

THE MAN. When?

THE WOMAN. With dad. My dad. My real dad was crap. Big. Distant. Non-verbal. Like a horse. Only things he liked were gin and fishing. Always drinking. Or catching fish. Basically avoiding us. Evening. Weekends. Eventually, one weekend, I thought fuck this. Got in the car. And we went fishing.

THE MAN. For trout.

THE WOMAN. Trout. Sea trout. Salmon.

THE MAN. How many times.

THE WOMAN. I'm really sorry.

THE MAN. How many times have you fished for sea trout?

THE WOMAN. A few times. Loads of times.

THE MAN. But on the beach. You couldn't cast. You couldn't tie a knot. Change a fly.

THE WOMAN. I faked it.

THE MAN. Why?

THE WOMAN. Because I fucking hate fishing. I always did. It was the only way I could get his attention. It's my tragedy in life that if I want to get a man to notice me, first I have to put on big rubber waders.

THE MAN. Why didn't you say?

THE WOMAN. You were having such fun. Teaching me to cast. Showing me all your bits and bobs. Suddenly we're not going fishing, I'm about to be shone upon by the light of eternity. Then Ted Hughes gets involved, and in the end I thought, fuck it, let's go catch a fish. Shut the poor sod up. (*Beat.*) You hate me. You want me to leave.

THE MAN. It wasn't a fluke.

THE WOMAN. I changed to a Black Bomber with three droppers.

THE MAN. You had three droppers?!

THE WOMAN. Not my idea. Dad's. If two isn't working…

THE MAN. What were they?

THE WOMAN. Sedgefield Yellow, a Black Gnat and a…

BOTH. Mallowflier.

THE WOMAN. Exactly.

THE MAN. You bastard…

THE WOMAN. Why the fuck not? In for a penny.

THE MAN. Well, it explains one thing.

THE WOMAN. What?

THE MAN. Why you didn't call. For help.

THE WOMAN. Are you kidding? Dad would have killed me.
The funniest thing happened. When it took, when the fish bit,
as it snatched the line and took off for the shallows, I saw
something.

THE MAN. What?

THE WOMAN. I saw Dad, dead on the kitchen floor. Naked. Not
dead. Dying. He had a seizure. I found him flip-flopping
frothing on the kitchen floor. I couldn't save him. I don't even
really remember it. Just how white he was. And how soft his
skin was. (*Pause*.) I lied to you. I feel like a complete fraud.

THE MAN. Don't.

THE WOMAN. Why not. I hid my borderline-expert ability to
catch wild fish in the dead of night. I mean that's why we're
here. That's the reason we came here.

THE MAN. Is that the reason we came here?

THE WOMAN. But you must be wondering.

THE MAN. Wondering what?

THE WOMAN. What else I've lied to you about.

THE MAN. I don't care.

THE WOMAN. Really?

THE MAN. Really.

THE WOMAN. Really? I wish I could stop saying 'really'.

THE MAN. I mean it.

THE WOMAN. And why's that.

THE MAN. This morning I woke up and you'd gone. I went outside looking for you. I couldn't see you anywhere. I went down the path to the river. And I walked about half a mile calling your name. And then I saw you. You were at the swimming hole. The water was high because of all the rain. And you stood on a boulder, twelve feet above the water. You stood there. Do you remember what you did next?

THE WOMAN. I took off all my clothes.

THE MAN. And you stood there completely naked. And then?

THE WOMAN. I dived into the water.

THE MAN. Into the freezing pool. And I watched you, from above, under the water, before you surfaced, and I said out loud to myself, 'Watch out. You're in trouble. You have to be as fearless and as honest as the thing you just saw happen. Because that's who you're dealing with. Now look out.'

Pause.

THE WOMAN. What you said this morning. When I got back from the river. In here. After we made love. Did you mean it? Wait you don't have to answer that.

THE MAN. I'll answer it.

THE WOMAN. No don't. You don't have to answer…

THE MAN. I meant it.

Beat.

THE WOMAN. No – Really? (*Beat.*) I don't want you to think because I didn't say it back –

THE MAN. I didn't expect you to –

THE WOMAN. Right. But I just… hope you didn't think because I didn't say it back –

THE MAN. I didn't think anything.

THE WOMAN. No but… I don't want you to think it's not that I'm not feeling that way. Not that I'm not open to it. Which as we've established is entirely different to being closed.

THE MAN. Entirely.

THE WOMAN. I think what I'm saying is I'm not not not… not open to it. I hope that's clear.

THE MAN. Perfectly.

THE WOMAN. Good. (*Beat*.) I thought it was a bit of a splashy dive to be honest.

THE MAN. It was a bit splashy.

THE WOMAN. It was a real face-stinger. I can still feel it.

THE MAN. I'm not surprised.

Pause.

THE WOMAN. Wow.

Silence.

So come on. Tell me something true. Something true about you.

THE MAN. What do you want to know.

Pause.

THE WOMAN. Tell me about the first fish you ever caught.

THE MAN. No.

THE WOMAN. Come on.

THE MAN. No, you fucking hate fishing.

THE WOMAN. Tell me anyway.

THE MAN. It was about five hundred yards from here. In the
    Long Pool. Past the swimming hole, past the rope swing.
    Where the bank hangs low above the black stones.

THE WOMAN. How old were you?

THE MAN. Seven. I was fishing after rain. It was cold. Still.
    The water gin-clear. My uncle was further up, fishing a wet
    fly beyond the crest. I was alone. Cold, bored, thinking about
    sausages, when out of nowhere the air thickened and
    yellowed, the wind changed and whipped up the surface like
    a million pinpricks, then stillness. Silence. And suddenly,
    under the beeches on the far bend. Where the black stones
    are. A single lapwing sedge, a tiny fly lit by sunlight, dipping
    low over the mirror water.

    And I blink and when I open my eyes… there's an explosion.
    A big fat trout, black-eyed. Tongue like a piece of blackboard
    chalk. Clears the water by three feet. Snaps its jaws shut on
    the poor fly and it's gone. Just the ripple, then silence. And my
    heart caves. My hands shake, blood beats in my balls. I kneel
    down and, sick, trembling, I cut off my fly and tie on the
    closest thing I can find to a lapwing. A tiny frozen shaking
    double reef knot. A schoolboy's knot. When I look up the river
    is a mirror. I can't see anything but upside-down trees and
    back-to-front sky. But just then a big chapel of cloud pushed
    overhead and there it was. A slow zigzag. Three feet beneath
    the surface. Thirty feet away. Out of the reach of my world-
    record cast. So quiet as I could I waded out into the faster
    water on this bank. Up to my waist. And I drew out some line
    and I cast about three feet short. Next cast lands two yards
    upstream from the last rise, and it drifts over the black stones
    and WHAM. The fish explodes up and rips my fly six feet
    down into the Long Pool. And the line goes slack. I've lost it.
    But then… Then the rod jerks in my hand like it's being pulled
    down by a fifty-pound weight. And the trout soars and flips out
    of the water and I have it. I've hooked this wild trout and it
    zinged out about fifty yards of line. My heart is beating in my
    cheeks, and my knees are thrumming like pneumatic drills, but
    I pay out the line. I keep the tip up. Keep tension but not too
    tight. And each time the line slackens I'm reeling in, and I

bring it off the black stones and into the net. And I wade back to the bank and fall to my knees and there it is. Flopping. Brown. Silver. Orange. Like a bar of precious metal. Like God's tongue. And I can't move. I just stare at it. And I know I've got to kill it. I know I've got to take my priest, my little truncheon, and smack its brains to eternity. (*Beat.*) But I can't. I just kneel there, panting, watching it pant. Both of us fighting for air. Thirty seconds. A minute. And as my breathing slows, so does its, until it goes still. And I reach forward and I lift it out of the net and it's floppy over my hands. And I hold it up to the light. And I close my eyes, shaking, and when I open my eyes. It's gone.

THE WOMAN. Gone?

THE MAN. I didn't even feel it flip. I didn't feel it leave my hands. But it must have found its last gram of life because all I felt was a shadow over the inside of my pink eyelids, and all I heard was a splash. It was gone. It was back. In the river. Alive. Swimming. Still alive. A miracle. And I crawled down the bank and I searched the water, deep into the water but all I could see down there was a small, seven-year-old boy gazing up at me, looking me straight in the eye, looking absolutely terrified. And I climbed up the bank and I sat in the bracken, alone, exhausted, and my uncle came up the bank and asked me what was wrong and... I cried. I don't know why. It wasn't because I lost my fish.

It was because I had seen something I never knew was there. A force. A spirit. I'd felt it buckle and shudder in my seven-year-old hands. And it thrilled me. And it scared the life out of me. Who knows why I was crying. It was all I could think to do. But I never, ever, ever forgot that feeling. And I try to describe it. But you can't. You can't describe it. There are no words. But I was there. And I felt it. (*Beat.*) My uncle said chin up. There's always tomorrow. You'll meet it again. Another day. And we came back here, and had sausages. And the next day I went back to the river, and I took off my clothes and I dived in the water, and I looked for the fish, and I couldn't find it, but when I surfaced, I was holding something. Something else.

THE WOMAN. What was it?

THE MAN. I still have it.

THE WOMAN. Where?

THE MAN. Next door. Under the bed. In an old hatbox. Under a stack of letters. Wrapped in a bottle-green handkerchief. Go and get it.

THE WOMAN. Why?

THE MAN. Because I want you to see it. I want to show you it. Go.

She gets up. She comes back.

THE WOMAN. Promise me it's not…

THE MAN. Not what?

THE WOMAN. Not a ring.

THE MAN. What?

THE WOMAN. Oh no.

THE MAN. It's not a ring.

THE WOMAN. Now I feel stupid. But incredibly. 'It's not a ring'… Honestly –

THE MAN. Relax. It's not a ring.

THE WOMAN. Is it a gun? Because I'd like to shoot myself right now.

THE MAN. It's not a gun. It's not a ring. It's something else.

THE WOMAN. What is it?

THE MAN. It's under the bed.

THE WOMAN. I'm scared.

THE MAN. Trust me.

She goes next door.

THE WOMAN. There's a box. I've got it.

THE MAN. Bring it here.

When she comes back…

She is the THE OTHER WOMAN.

Open it.

THE OTHER WOMAN. Are you sure?

THE MAN. I'm sure.

She opens it. It's a black stone. The size and shape of a heart.

THE OTHER WOMAN. It's beautiful.

THE MAN. No one else has ever seen it. I've never shown it to anyone. I want you to have it.

THE OTHER WOMAN. I can't.

THE MAN. Please… Take it.

Pause.

THE OTHER WOMAN. When I came back earlier, there was a robin in here. Tiny bird. I opened all the windows but I forgot to open that one up high and it flew right into it. It fell right here on the floor.

THE MAN. Was it dead?

THE OTHER WOMAN. I don't know. I took it outside. I put it on the wall. I forgot to check if it's still there.

THE MAN. It's happened before. It will be fine.

THE OTHER WOMAN. I hope so. Poor thing.

Beat.

Darkness. The river.

Some music is playing in the cabin. THE WOMAN *comes in wrapped in a towel. Towelling her hair.*

THE MAN. How do you like the shower?

THE WOMAN. Amazing. So refreshing. Yeah. God. (*Beat.*) Actually it's freezing.

THE MAN. You mean bracing.

THE WOMAN. I mean arse-bitingly cold.

THE MAN. But the view.

THE WOMAN. The view is breathtaking. The shower is hell.
Freezing hell. I can't feel anything south of my tits.

THE MAN. Did you wiggle the knob?

THE WOMAN. I wiggled the knob. It just got ten times colder.
So I turned it all the way round the other way.

THE MAN. I said. Don't turn it the other way –

THE WOMAN. I panicked.

THE MAN. I specifically said. Where is it?

THE WOMAN. On the windowsill. Next to the brass soap dish.
With the soap. And the pair of gold earrings.

Pause.

THE MAN. What?

THE WOMAN. There's a pair of gold earrings in the soap dish.
Next to the soap.

Silence.

THE MAN. Okay –

THE WOMAN. You don't have to say anything. Really. It's
none of my business. I mean –

THE MAN. Listen –

THE WOMAN. It's no big deal.

THE MAN. Sit down. Please –

THE WOMAN. After all, we're both adults. We can be honest
with each other. Can't we? I mean, can't we?

Silence.

Today on the beach, you were teaching me to cast. And I
asked you, as a joke, I think… just being silly, who knows

why, I asked how many other women you'd brought here. To this place. And you went quiet. You picked up a stone. So for fun, or for some other reason, some deadly serious reason, or just playing, who knows, I said come on, give me a number. I don't know why. I mean what does it matter? If I'm the third, fourth, seventh, eighth. What difference does it make? (*Beat.*) But I asked. (*Beat.*) And you looked me straight in the eye and said do you really want to know? And it all went silent out there on the beach and the sea was coming in I looked back at you and I was suddenly afraid. I suddenly, desperately, urgently didn't want to know. But I said yes. Tell me. (*Pause.*) And you told me. (*Beat.*) And I said come on. In all these years. Come off it. I wasn't born yesterday. (*Beat.*) And you said it's true. (*Beat.*) Afterwards, in this room we made love. When it was over, you said something. You told me something. Words which completely surprised me and scared me. And I've thought of nothing else since.

THE MAN. Yes.

Pause.

THE WOMAN. This morning you said you came to the river, and you watched me dive in the water. You said it was the most honest thing you'd ever seen and you realised you had to be as honest and truthful as that moment.

THE MAN. Yes.

THE WOMAN. That you would always try to be that.

THE MAN. Yes.

THE WOMAN. Hanging in the cupboard next door is a dress. A scarlet dress. Under the bed, in the box there's a framed picture. A drawing of a woman. She's sitting there in that chair. She's wearing a scarlet dress. The woman in the picture. Her face has been scratched out.

Silence.

Why is her face scratched out? (*Pause.*) Why is her dress still here?

A voice off, singing the tune to 'The Song of Wandering Aengus'.

THE WOMAN *and* THE MAN *stand staring at one another.*

Enter THE OTHER WOMAN. *Wearing a scarlet dress.*

She pours water from a jug into a bowl and lights candles around it, humming the tune.

While THE OTHER WOMAN *performs the ritual, all the time humming the tune,* THE WOMAN *goes into the bedroom.*

THE OTHER WOMAN *sits in front of him.* THE MAN *is drawing her.*

THE OTHER WOMAN. So come on. So who invented it? Fly-fishing. Who thought it up?

THE MAN. 'There is a river called Astraeus, which floweth midway between Berea and Thessalonica – '

THE OTHER WOMAN. Are you quoting now. Is this a quote?

THE MAN. ' – in which are produced certain spotted fish – '

THE OTHER WOMAN. Oh God it is –

THE MAN. ' – whose food consists of insects which fly above the river – '

THE OTHER WOMAN. This is serious isn't it. I mean, it's a real fucking problem.

THE MAN. When a fish espies one –

THE OTHER WOMAN. 'Espies'...

THE MAN. ' – it swimmeth quiet beneath, taking care to agitate not the surface lest it should fright its prey. The fishermen of the Astraeus, thus observing, cover a hook with red wool, and upon this they fasten two feathers of waxy appearance, which grow under cock wattles. They have a reed six feet long, they drop the lure upon the water, and the fish, attracted by the form, movement and colour becomes excited, proceeds to meet it, anticipating from its beautiful appearance a most delicious repast, but, as with extended mouth it seizes the lure and it is held fast by the hook, and being captured meets with its death.'

THE OTHER WOMAN. Where did you pick that up?

THE MAN. The writings of Aelian, mid-third century. Christian era. Think about it. Most fishing is chucking in real food on a line and the fish gobbles it up. It's too easy. There's nothing real about this. This is entirely artificial. It's trickery. It's a trick.

He draws.

THE OTHER WOMAN. You're not looking at me.

THE MAN. That's because I'm not drawing you.

THE OTHER WOMAN. Then what are you drawing.

THE MAN. I'm drawing your reflection. Before mirrors, this was the only way we could see ourselves. Reflected in water. (*Beat.*) Can you see me? Hello.

THE OTHER WOMAN. Hello. (*Beat.*) So what's the difference between a trout and a sea trout?

THE MAN. Nothing. There's no difference. Not to start with. To start with they're all just trout. Brown trout. In the river. As they all grow up, go to school, all the brown trout find their spot on the river, their turf, and they defend it against other fish. Now some trout, the weakest trout, they go down the river looking for a spot, getting beaten up by all the other bigger fish. And they keep on looking till they get to the sea. And they go out to sea, and get eaten by bigger fish. Except some survive. They swim up to Iceland. The furthest Norwegian fjord. And they change. The sea changes them. They go from brown to silver, the very shape of their skulls changes and they grow very very big. Then when late summer comes, when it comes time to spawn, they go back home, back up the river, bigger, stronger, and now they can go anywhere. Now it's payback time. They beat up all the bully-boy brown trout who only last year were beating them up. A trout, a brown trout, lives only in freshwater. Whereas your sea trout migrates. Unlike your salmon which spawns once and dies, your sea trout go back to the sea, get bigger, and next year do it all over again. Unless they get caught. Suddenly. In the middle of the night.

Pause.

THE OTHER WOMAN. Can I have some more wine?

THE MAN. Of course.

He gets up. Fills her glass.

THE OTHER WOMAN. I wonder what else this water has reflected. Other faces. Other men. Women. This same water. The sunrise. The sunset. A million times. From cups. Buckets. It was water in a river, a thousand years ago, reflecting the rain falling onto it. It was the rain falling on to the river, falling on to its own reflection, as it touches itself and becomes the river. (*Beat.*) Has it seen you before? Your face, your shape, as you dived into it. As a boy. Did it watch you, fishing the river. Fighting your first trout. Or was it the tears you wept on the bank, after it had gone.

How's it going. Are you capturing me?

THE MAN. We're getting somewhere.

THE OTHER WOMAN. I always find pictures and photographs unbearably sad.

THE MAN. Why's that?

THE OTHER WOMAN. Because here we are now, in this room, but in five, ten, twenty years, you will find this picture in a cupboard, perhaps here, perhaps somewhere else, somewhere you've not yet been, in the corner of an attic under boxes of old hammers and chisels, and you'll dust it off and think, who is that? I know that face. Whose face is that. Perhaps you'll come to this place, an old man, seventy, eighty years old, you will come here to catch sea trout, and one night, alone, as you're going to bed, you'll see this picture. And you'll carry it to the window. The sun will be setting. And you will think when did this happen? Was it summer? Who is that woman? So many years, you can't recall. And you'll put the picture back in the box, and that night, you lie down, and stare into the dark, and you will try to remember. How you felt. You'll try to be back there. To live it again. But you can't get back there. You can never go back. May I ask you a question?

THE MAN. Of course.

THE OTHER WOMAN. How many women have you brought here.

THE MAN. You really want to know? (*Pause*.) When I was about twelve my uncle said he'd brought lots and lots of women here. Fillies he called them. And he said how he used to do the same things with each of them. The same routine. He'd bring them here around sunset, pour them a large scotch. Take them fishing then bring them back and quote have his wicked way. He said he'd brought dozens here. So many he said he'd get them mixed up. Have to write down their names. And he laughed. He laughed that big laugh of his. But he suddenly had the eyes of a ghost. And the mouth of some desperate creature caught in an invisible snare. As I went to sleep that night I promised myself I would only bring one woman here. The woman I wanted to spend my life with. The woman I wanted to be with for ever. She would come here, and it would be sacred. It would be something I had only shared with her and her alone.

Silence.

Earlier this evening, when you came back. I said something to you. And you laughed it off.

THE OTHER WOMAN. I wouldn't say I laughed it off.

THE MAN. It's okay. You were surprised. Not as surprised as me. Trust me, I didn't want to say it. But I had no choice. Because there was nothing else in my head or in my whole being. There was no way forward except through that. There was no next breath without it. And you're right. I may forget who you are. I may bring other women here, to this place, and I may tell them I love them, and make love to them. But they will be imposters. And I will be a ghost. Because it means I will have lost you. My body, my brain, my lungs, my stomach, my guts, legs, arms will be here but I won't be. I will be out there, looking for you. And if we meet somewhere, at a restaurant, or a party and I'm with someone, I want you to know that they are by my side only because you are not. And she will be beautiful. And I will be laughing and smiling and she will be laughing and smiling, but she will be laughing at a lie. Because all I will have done to that person is lie to them. All I will do to anyone else, forever, from this moment forward, anyone who isn't you, is lie. I have no choice. (*Beat.*) I have no choice.

Silence.

THE OTHER WOMAN. This afternoon I was reading in here, alone. Curled up over there, completely lost. And you came up behind me and do you remember what you did.

THE MAN. I kissed your neck.

THE OTHER WOMAN. You kissed the back of my neck. It was so gentle. And light shone all down my spine and into my tummy. I forgot what I'd been reading. What language it was in. What I'd done all week. How I even got here. Like I could drop the book, and kick and buck for joy. And I thought one single burning thought. I want to eat him whole. Every inch of him. Now. And I pulled you next door. And we tore off our clothes and I lay you down and it felt like each split second had already happened and was perfect and coming and done all at once. And suddenly you were beneath me, and inside me. It was beyond hunger, beyond need. Like this giant rolling fiery roaring ball with me in the middle of it, like at that moment I was the only woman in the world. And you were the only man. I looked into your eyes. Deep into your eyes, with you inside me, with us together, alone, here, just us, I gazed into your eyes. (*Pause.*) And you looked away.

Silence.

And I took your face. And I turned it back to face mine. And again you looked away. I said your name. You screwed your eyes tight, and tensed your jaw, and flinched, and shuddered. And your skin went cold. Your breath turned sour. And your hands felt small. You flipped me over, and got on top of me, and you drove your face into the pillow and thirty seconds later it was over. And we lay there in silence. And you stood up, and came in here, and three minutes later you reappeared with two cups of strong tea, and you put them down on either side of the bed, and you asked me if the tea was okay. If that's how I liked it. I said it was perfect. It was just right. (*Pause*.) Then the sun set. And we went to the river.

Pause.

THE MAN. Look at us. In this place. We're the only ones here. Just us. Here. Now. Together. I'm with you. Only you. You have to believe me. Please. Please believe me.

THE OTHER WOMAN. Keep looking at me. Now. In my eyes. Don't look away. Look into my eyes.

He does. She holds his gaze.

You love me.

THE MAN. I love you.

THE OTHER WOMAN. This is your heart speaking.

THE MAN. Only my heart.

THE OTHER WOMAN. If you lose me you will search for me. For ever.

THE MAN. For ever.

Beat.

THE OTHER WOMAN. Next door. Under the bed, in the box there's a framed drawing. A drawing of a woman. She's sitting here in this chair. She's wearing a scarlet dress. Her face has been scratched out.

He holds her gaze. Slowly. He looks away.

She goes in to the bedroom. She reappears with her small suitcase.

Pause.

THE MAN. Please. Don't go.

She looks at him. She approaches, kisses him on the forehead.

THE OTHER WOMAN. I hope you find her. Whoever she is.

Pause.

She leaves.

Silence.

THE WOMAN *enters from the bedroom. With her suitcase.*

Silence.

THE MAN. I'll drive you to the station.

THE WOMAN. If it's the same I'd like to walk.

THE MAN. It's four miles.

THE WOMAN. I'm perfectly capable of walking four miles.

THE MAN. The first train isn't till seven-thirty.

THE WOMAN. I'll wait in the waiting room.

THE MAN. There isn't a waiting room.

THE WOMAN. Then I'll wait on the platform.

THE MAN. Well then –

THE WOMAN. What happened to her? (*Pause.*) She's dead.

Isn't she?

That's it isn't it.

She died.

Silence. He shakes his head.

Pause.

Then what happened to her?

Silence.

Where did she go? (*Pause.*) Did she even exist?

Silence. He looks at her.

THE MAN. Yesterday in this room after we made love I said something to you.

THE WOMAN. You said you loved me.

THE MAN. And you blushed and you laughed and you looked at the floor and then out of the window and you sighed and said something. Do you remember what you said?

THE WOMAN. I can't remember.

THE MAN. Yes you can.

THE WOMAN. I can't remember.

THE MAN. Try. Try to remember.

THE WOMAN. I said. I'm –

BOTH. – not entirely sure what love is.

Silence.

THE MAN. Those are the first true words we have said to each other. The only true words we have ever spoken. (*Pause.*) You can go now.

Silence.

THE WOMAN. I believed you. And last night, when we talked, in here, alone, I felt I understood something about myself for the first time. It's like in that one moment I suddenly could see all around myself and place myself and see where I was going, and where I'd been… and it felt wonderful. I felt… I felt like from this moment forward anything could happen. Anything… (*Pause.*) Here.

She takes the stone out and drops it on the floor. He looks at it, lying there on the floor.

She leaves.

A VOICE (*singing*).

> I went out to a hazel wood
> Because a fire was in my head
> And cut and peeled a hazel wand
> And hooked a berry to a thread
> And when white moths were on the wing
> And moth-like stars were flickering out
> I dropped the berry in the stream
> And caught a little silver trout...

He goes over to the stone. He picks it up. Looks at it.

Silence.

As the singing continues, he picks up the stone. Wraps it up. He notices the bowl of water.

He fetches the bowl of water.

He looks at his reflection in the bowl.

> When I had laid it on the floor
> I went to blow the fire aflame
> But something rustled on the floor
> And someone called me by my name
> It had become a glimmering girl
> With apple blossom in her hair
> Who called me by my name and ran
> And faded through the brightening air.

The sun rises.

> Though I am old and wandering
> Through hollow lands and hilly lands
> I will find out where she has gone
> And kiss her lips and takes her hands
> And walk among long dappled grass
> And pluck till time and times are done
> The silver apples of the moon
> The golden apples of the sun.

Enter ANOTHER WOMAN. *He doesn't turn to look at her.*

THE MAN. Where have you been?

ANOTHER WOMAN. I've been down to the river. The sun is rising.

THE MAN. I looked for you. I looked for you everywhere. I couldn't find you.

ANOTHER WOMAN. I went to the Long Pool. It's absolutely teeming with fish. Shoals of them, gliding in the clear water. They're so beautiful. I reached my hand in and fifty scattered in an instant. (*Beat.*) Are you sure I'm going to catch one?

He turns and looks at her. Silence.

THE MAN. I have something to show you. Something I've never shown anyone before.

They stand opposite each other in silence.

Darkness.

The End.